Don't miss any of the titles
in the ALIEN INVADERS series:

ROCKHEAD: THE LIVING MOUNTAIN
INFERNOX: THE FIRESTARTER
ZILLAH: THE FANGED PREDATOR
HYDRONIX: DESTROYER OF THE DEEP
ATOMIC: THE RADIOACTIVE BOMB
KRUSH: THE IRON GIANT
JUNKJET: THE FLYING MENACE
MINOX: THE PLANET DRILLER
ZIPZAP: THE REBEL RACER
TANKA: THE BALLISTIC BLASTER

ALIEN INVADERS: KRUSH, THE IRON GIANT
A RED FOX BOOK 978 1 849 41235 3

First published in Great Britain by Red Fox,
an imprint of Random House Children's Books
A Random House Group Company

This edition published 2012

3 5 7 9 10 8 6 4 2

Text and illustrations copyright © David Sinden,
Guy Macdonald and Matthew M...
Cover and inte..Design

The Random .... ip
Council (FSC®), ... tion.
Our books car .... er.
FSC is the o... ¿
envir¿...
Ou........................ ...¿y can be found at
www.randomhouse.co.uk/environment

MIX
Paper from
responsible sources
FSC   FSC® C016897
www.fsc.org

Set in Century Schoolbook

Red Fox Books are published by
Random House Children's Books, 61–63 Uxbridge Road, London W5 5SA

www.**kids**at**randomhouse**.co.uk
www.**randomhouse**.co.uk

Addresses for companies within The Random House Group Limited can be
found at: www.randomhouse.co.uk/offices.htm

THE RANDOM HOUSE GROUP Limited Reg. No. 954009

A CIP catalogue record for this book is available from
the British Library.

Printed and bound by CPI Group (UK) Ltd,
Croydon, CR0 4YY

ALIEN INVADERS

MAX SILVER

KRUSH
THE IRON GIANT

RED FOX

THE GALAXY

Cosmo's route - - - -

DELTA QUADRANT

GAMMA QUADRANT

STARFLIGHT SPACESHIP
MANUFACTURING COMPANY

PLANET SYN-NOVA

PLANET BALAZ

SYSTEM OPEX

ALPHA QUADRANT

MOON OF GARR

GALACTIC CORE

BETA QUADRANT

THE WRECKING ZONE

PLANET KEFU

RESISTANCE IS FUTILE, EARTHLINGS!

MY NAME IS KAOS, AND MY WAR WITH YOUR GALAXY IS ENTERING A NEW PHASE...

THE YEAR IS 2121 AND I HAVE JOINED FORCES WITH METALLICON ALIENS FROM A DEAD-SPACE WILDERNESS KNOWN AS THE WRECKING ZONE. THEY HAVE THE POWER OF LIVING MACHINES, AND I AM PROGRAMMING THEM TO INVADE YOUR GALAXY.

YOUR SECURITY FORCE, G-WATCH, WILL BE POWERLESS TO DEFEND YOU, AND ITS EARTHLING AGENT, COSMO SANTOS, WILL BE ANNIHILATED ALONG WITH HIS FRIENDS.

RESISTANCE IS FUTILE, EARTHLINGS. THE GALAXY WILL BE MINE!

INVADER ALERT!

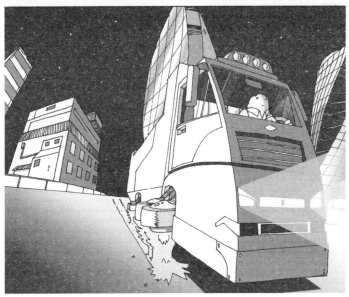

On Planet Syn-Nova, construction worker
Hans Lopus drove between newly built
offices and skyscrapers, the headlights of
his Planetrax transporter-crane shining
through the darkness. He held the wheel
with his long-fingered Mucon hands,
powering along a recently laid city street,
working the night shift. He had a heavy
load on board, a shiny new eco-solar dish to
be installed on one of Syn-Nova's towers.

Pulling up beside a tall glass building, Hans pressed a button on the transporter-crane's control panel, and a split-screen monitor flickered into life. It displayed two different views of the vehicle's trailer, showing the positions of its crane arm and the eco-solar dish.

Hans flicked a switch, engaging the crane arm. With a joystick he manoeuvred the hook at its end, attaching it with a *clunk!* to the solar dish. The transporter's crane arm reached upwards on its telescopic extenders, hoisting the solar dish to the top of the tall glass building and slotting it neatly into position on the roof.

All night, Hans and other workers had been busy installing solar dishes around Syn-Nova. In the morning, the dishes would begin capturing the sun's rays, converting them into useable energy for the new state-of-the-art city planet.

Hans opened his window and glanced

up at the night, breathing the purified air. He smiled; it was still a while until sunrise and he was on target to finish in time – it was Syn-Nova's grand opening in the morning and everything had to be ready.

High in the sky, among the shimmer of the planet's atmospheric shield, Hans spotted an object speeding downwards.

Is that a skytrain bringing the first batch of Syn-Nova's new residents already? he thought. Hans frowned doubtfully. *It can't be. It's still too early.* He gasped as the object hurtled lower, coming in fast in his direction! It grew larger as it neared, showing no sign of stopping. It appeared to be some kind of monster machine!

With a *boom!* it crashed down on the building with the eco-solar dish, blasting glass and metal across the street. Debris clattered against the transporter-crane, and the air filled with dust. Hans stared, rigid with shock, as the dust settled.

Where the building had been destroyed, a freakish machine-like alien rose from the wreckage. It was the yellow colour of a construction vehicle and moved like an iron giant, smoke pumping from exhaust pipes on its back. Instead of hands it had a huge metal claw and a wrecking ball on a chain. With angry red eyes it stared down at Hans, then swung the wrecking ball, smashing it onto the transporter-crane's trailer. Next it reached down with its claw and picked up the transporter-crane like a toy.

"Heeeeeelp!" Hans cried. With a sickening *crunch!* he felt the alien smash the vehicle down hard, breaking open a hole in the street.

Hans slid across his cab, knocking his head against the window. He felt himself losing consciousness, everything going black as the alien roared, "I am Krush! Destroy! Destroy! DESTROY!"

CHAPTER ONE

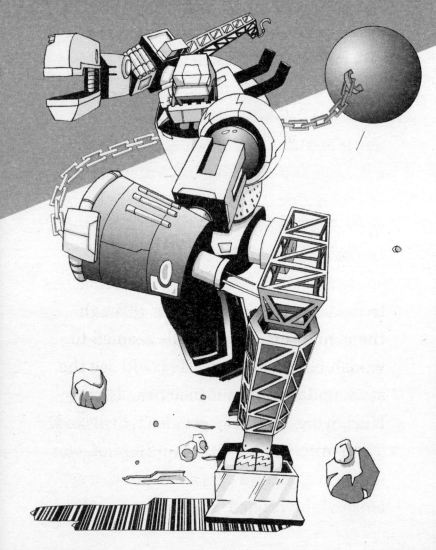

A BRAND NEW MISSION

In the cockpit of the Dragster 7000 spaceship, Cosmo tried on a pair of goggles from the kit shelf. He looked through them, and the cockpit walls seemed to vanish before his eyes. He could see the stars and planets out in space. "Hey, Nuri, what are these goggles?" he asked.

Agent Nuri, his Etrusian co-pilot, was at the spaceship's controls. "They're spy lenses," she replied, smiling.

Cosmo could see through her blue skin to her skeleton. *Like X-ray specs*, he thought. *Cool!*

Brain-E, the ship's bug-like brainbot, bleeped from the control desk. "The Dragster's kit has been replenished for your new mission, Master Cosmo," it said.

Cosmo pushed up the spy lenses and checked out other gadgets among the kit: magnetized climbing boots, a jet-powered snowboard, gravity grenades, a muscle maximizer armband, an eagle eyescope . . .

Cosmo Santos, an eleven-year-old Earthling boy, was on a brand-new mission for the galactic security force G-Watch. He had already saved the galaxy from invaders from the Doom Vortex, and was now off to face five new enemies being beamed into the galaxy by the outlaw Kaos. They would be fearsome opponents: aliens half living and half machine that had evolved in a deep-space dumping ground called the Wrecking Zone.

Cosmo had been chosen for the mission because of a power he possessed inside – the power of the universe, present in all living things but uniquely strong in him. It activated G-Watch's most advanced fighting tool, the Quantum Mutation Suit, the spacesuit that could transform Cosmo into alien life forms to battle his enemies.

A light flashed on the communications console, and Cosmo sat in the Dragster's pilot's seat and flicked a switch. On the ship's monitor he saw the silver eyes and green skin of G1, the Chief of G-Watch.

"The invasion has begun, team," G1 said. "We've received scanner data signalling a strike on Planet Syn-Nova in the Gamma Quadrant."

"We're ready," Cosmo replied confidently.

"Cosmo, you will need to select your mutations wisely," G1 warned him. "The aliens from the Wrecking Zone are unlike any other life forms in the universe. They are resilient, adaptable and, above all, deadly. According to our scanners, the first to have been sent is the iron giant known as Krush."

Cosmo gulped. "An iron giant?" *I don't like the sound of that*, he thought.

"Good luck, Cosmo. The galaxy is grateful to you for your courage."

The monitor went blank as G1 ended the communication.

"You're not going to let a tin can called Krush beat you, are you?" Nuri asked.

"Of course not," Cosmo replied, trying to appear unfazed.

But Brain-E bleeped worriedly. "G1's warning was for good reason, Master Cosmo: this mission will be a true test of your powers. These aliens, known as metallicons, have evolved from the fusion of metallic bacterial sludge and machine debris. They are uniquely dangerous."

Cosmo glanced at Nuri apprehensively.

"We're a team, Cosmo," Nuri told him

defiantly. "One of the best. And we're not going down without a fight."

Cosmo smiled, glad that Nuri and Brain-E were with him. "Then let's go!"

Nuri programmed the route co-ordinates and words lit up on the spacescreen:

```
DESTINATION: SYN-NOVA
DISTANCE: 3.55 BILLION MILES
STAR SYSTEM: POLARK, GAMMA QUADRANT
ROUTE: HYPERWAY 98 FROM AURILO NEBULA
```

Cosmo blasted the Dragster through space towards a distant cluster of stars, the Aurilo Nebula. The spacescreen

turned pink and green as the ship passed through the nebula's plasma, then Cosmo pulled hard on the steering column and banked between a line of blinking space beacons onto Hyperway 98. He engaged hyperdrive, shooting the Dragster across the galaxy at twice the speed of light.

"So, Cosmo, how does it feel to be the new Agent Supreme?" Nuri asked.

Cosmo had been awarded G-Watch's highest rank of Agent Supreme when he had completed his first mission, stopping the outlaw Kaos's attempt to take over the galaxy. "It feels cool," he replied. "I only wish my dad could see me now."

Cosmo's father, who'd been a G-Watch agent himself, had died in a space-crash just over two years earlier. "Kaos said he knew my father, Nuri. How come?"

"Because Kaos was once a G-Watch agent too, Cosmo," Nuri replied. "Then, a few years ago, he was caught stealing top-secret G-Watch data, including the blueprints for navicom transporter units and the locations of dangerous species beyond our galaxy. He defected, fleeing in a G-Watch battleship and declaring war."

"Kaos once belonged to G-Watch! *Really?*"

"He sure did. But now he wants G-Watch finished so he can take control of the galaxy for himself."

Cosmo looked ahead at the streaking lights of hyperspace. He had seen what destruction Kaos and his invaders were capable of. "We've stopped him once and we'll stop him again," he said resolutely. "How much further to Syn-Nova?"

"Exit hyperdrive in eleven Earth seconds," Nuri replied.

Cosmo counted down then veered off the hyperway into open space. A single bright star shone ahead in the blackness. Cosmo tapped the spacescreen, activating its star plotter again, and a name appeared beside the star: POLARK. Orbiting the star was a small planet labelled SYN-NOVA. As he took the Dragster nearer, the planet seemed to ripple, and he noticed a jelly-like membrane surrounding its atmosphere. "Brain-E, what's that around Syn-Nova?" he asked.

"It's an atmospheric shield, Master, that stops Syn-Nova's air supply evaporating into space. Syn-Nova is an engineered planet, built to help with population expansion in the Gamma Quadrant. It is to be home to a new supercity."

Cosmo had heard of engineered planets in Space Studies lessons back at school on Earth. They were said to be the future for space living – planets that could be built wherever they were needed and that could run entirely self-sufficiently using the latest technologies.

He reduced speed, steering the Dragster

through the jelly-like atmospheric shield, then switched to planetary mode, emerging into a night sky. He checked the external gauges:

PLENTIFUL OXYGEN ... TEMPERATURE TWENTY DEGREES CENTIGRADE ... GRAVITY: 0.2 ABOVE ZERO

Down he flew towards the planet's surface, the lights of a city like pinpricks far below. At 2,000 metres he flew past a large floating platform where a fleet of shiny new skytrains was docked.

A warning flashed on the spacescreen:

DOCK-AND-RIDE ZONE!

"What's Dock-and-Ride, Brain-E?"

"Dock-and-Ride is a space traffic system designed to avoid congestion in the new city below," Brain-E replied. "Citizens are to dock their spaceships up here, then take the skytrains to travel around Syn-Nova. It is strictly forbidden for spaceships to fly low over the city."

"Well, we don't have time to take a

train just now," Cosmo said. He switched on the Dragster's searchlights and zoomed down over the city.

Nuri checked the navigation console. "According to G-Watch scanner data, Krush has struck due west of here," she said.

Cosmo adjusted course, flying above glittering skyscrapers, then swooped between the levels of a multi-lane hoverway and over an elevated river.

"Cosmo, down there!" Nuri said, pointing to a demolished building below.

Cosmo banked, circling the Dragster lower. He shone its searchlights on a huge chasm in the ground and saw a construction vehicle wedged deep down inside it among crisscrossing iron girders. "I'm taking us in to land," he said. "Keep on your guard for Krush. He might still be nearby."

CHAPTER TWO

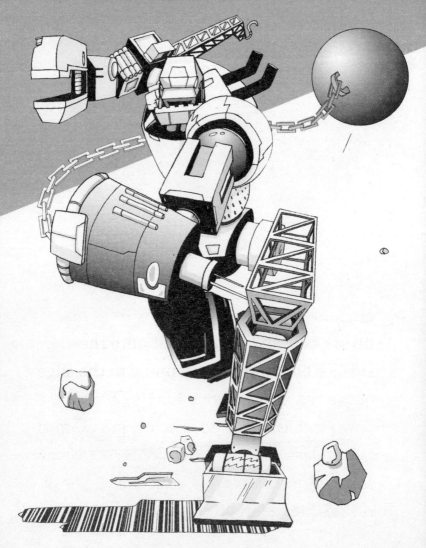

AN ENDLESS DROP

The Dragster landed and Cosmo put on
his helmet then opened the cockpit door.
He unclipped a plasma torch from his
utility belt and jumped out onto the
surface of Syn-Nova. Stepping to the edge
of the chasm, he shone his torchbeam
down into the ground. The chasm seemed
bottomless and revealed the structure of
the engineered planet: a surface layer of
rocks, then a supporting latticework of

crisscrossing steel girders, and below that, metal columns plunging to the planet's dark centre. Wedged among the girders, about thirty metres down, lay the wreck of a transporter-crane. Cosmo could just make out a driver at its controls. "Hello-o-o-o," Cosmo called down, his voice echoing. "Can you hear me-me-me?"

There was no reply.

"Nuri, the driver's down there. I'm going to get him out," Cosmo said into his helmet mic.

Nuri came out of the Dragster carrying the magnetic boots from the kit shelf and handed them to Cosmo. "These might help you," she said.

"Good thinking," Cosmo replied.

He swapped the boots of his Quantum Mutation Suit for the magnetic boots, then climbed into the chasm.

Cosmo carefully clambered down past the rocks to the network of metal girders. Stepping to one of them, he felt his left boot clamp on firmly, holding him steady. He lifted his right boot onto it, and that gripped too. The boots were sensitive to the motion of his body; he could release

them with a stepping motion but secure them magnetically each time he put a foot down. Step by step he descended into the darkness, ducking under humming power cables and gurgling water pipes. His footsteps echoed, their sound falling away into the vast drop below. He wondered how far he'd fall if he slipped: *A mile? Ten miles? A hundred miles?* The drop looked endless. *As long as these boots hold firm, I'll be OK*, he told himself.

Suddenly Cosmo heard a wrenching sound as the transporter-crane slid a few metres lower. He had to hurry.

His heart raced as he stepped onto a long metal column and leaned forward, walking vertically down it with his body facing the great drop below. He shone his torch and saw that the driver inside the cab was unconscious, his head bleeding and his eyes closed. Cosmo approached, and the transporter-crane tilted and slipped again. *It's falling!* he realized. Quickly he heaved open its cab door and pulled the driver out.

"What's going on?" the man asked, dazed, his eyelids flickering and opening.

With a screech, the transporter-crane plummeted away into darkness, clattering off metal columns on its descent to the planet's core.

Cosmo held onto the driver. "Are you OK?" he asked him.

The man looked around, petrified. "Where am I?"

"You're underground. You're safe now."

"Cosmo, are you alive?" Nuri called over the communicator.

"Yes, I'm coming up!" he replied into his helmet's mic. He unclipped a grappling gun from his utility belt and, holding the injured driver tightly, shot up a thin steel cable with a grappling hook at its end. The hook dug into the planet's surface rock, and Cosmo hit the retractor button, hoisting them both upwards. Nuri reached down and helped the driver the last few metres up to the surface.

"Thanks, kid," the driver said to Cosmo. "You saved my life."

"All in the line of duty," Cosmo told him. "We're from G-Watch. I'm Agent Cosmo. This is Agent Nuri."

"Pleased to meet you," the man replied. "I'm Hans Lopus. I work for Planetrax. I was installing a solar dish, getting Syn-Nova operational before the new citizens arrive in the morning, when a freak alien crashed down. It was huge – like a living machine!"

Cosmo shone his torch onto the cracks in a wide road leading off between the buildings. "Looks like he strode off in that direction," he said.

Suddenly there came a rumbling sound from overhead and Cosmo shone his torch upwards, half expecting to see Krush bearing down on them. Instead, a skytrain whizzed through the sky between the buildings, streaking eastwards, the same direction that Krush had gone. "How come skytrains are flying if the planet's not operational yet?" Cosmo asked.

"That'll be the first of the new residents moving into the city," Hans Lopus replied.

"Moving in?"

"Yes, it's Syn-Nova's official opening in the morning. There's going to be a ceremony in the city centre with the new mayor of Syn-Nova arriving, and thousands of people coming to celebrate."

So that's why Krush is striking here

now, Cosmo thought, alarmed. He watched the skytrain as it disappeared beyond the buildings. *Only a few hours and Krush will be stomping straight into a crowded city centre.* "Let's go, Nuri. We've no time to lose," he said. He quickly changed back into his Quantum Mutation Suit boots, about to head off.

"Wait a second – where's Brain-E?" Nuri asked.

Cosmo and Nuri shone their torches looking for the little brainbot, but there was no sign of it anywhere.

Cosmo spoke into his helmet's communicator: "Brain-E, where are you? Come in, Brain-E!"

With a loud *honk!* and flash of headlights a massive Planetrax MAXI-truck with huge wheels came trundling along the road out of the darkness. In its cab, next to the driver, Cosmo spotted tiny coloured lights blinking from the dashboard. "Nuri, it's Brain-E!"

The truck parked up, and the brainbot called down from its window, "I've found us some transport."

The truck's Mucon driver climbed down from the cab. "This truck's all yours; your robot friend explained the situation," he said to Cosmo. "I'll call for back-up for Hans here and get him to safety."

"Wow! I've always wanted to drive a MAXI-truck!" Cosmo said. While the driver attended to Hans Lopus, Cosmo and Nuri both clambered up to the MAXI's cab.

"Good work, Brain-E," Nuri said.

Brain-E bleeped. "With skytrains arriving, flying the Dragster around Syn-Nova will be too dangerous, so I thought we'd need a suitable land vehicle to go in search of our enemy."

Cosmo sat in the driver's seat high off the ground and gripped the wide steering wheel. "This is brilliant, Brain-E." He flicked the ignition switch and the engine throbbed loudly, making the whole cab tremble. He slipped the

truck into gear, and its mighty wheels all turned at once, speeding them on their way. "Let's go get Krush!"

CHAPTER THREE

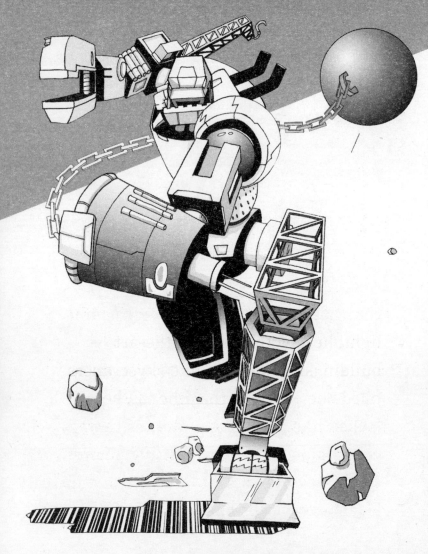

A TRAIL OF DESTRUCTION

Dawn was just breaking as Cosmo drove
the MAXI-truck east towards the city
centre in pursuit of Krush. In the dim
light, he saw the state-of-the-art
buildings. Some were like skyscrapers
piled one on top of the other. Others
looked like pinnacles and interlinking
boxes joined at strange jutting angles.
He drove onto an avenue between multi-
level hoverblocks and the highest

buildings he had ever seen. The road
rose to a sloping bridge then an elevated
public concourse, and overhead the
tubular river snaked among the buildings.

Syn-Nova is the coolest city ever! Cosmo
thought.

The road spiralled around the
buildings, rising and dipping, bending
and weaving. Cosmo saw something
large and metallic up ahead, and braked
quickly, thinking it was Krush. The
MAXI's headlights revealed a hydraulic
digger lying on its side, squashed.
"Krush has definitely come this way,"
Cosmo said as he drove past it, glancing
to check that its driver had escaped
unharmed.

The MAXI-truck's tyres crunched over
broken glass and he looked up and saw a
tall glass building with big holes
punched in its side.

"Thank goodness no one's living in

this part of the city yet," Nuri said, staring up at the demolition. But at that moment another skytrain thundered overhead, weaving between the buildings, taking more new citizens to the city centre. Sunlight was seeping into the sky and it was getting lighter by the minute.

"It'll be morning soon, and time for Syn-Nova's official opening," Cosmo said. "We have to stop Krush before he reaches the city centre."

He sped down a wide avenue and at the end saw a mangled metal wind turbine over fifty metres tall, its twisted blades rotating, clanging noisily.

Brain-E bleeped. "The wind turbines on Syn-Nova provide more renewable energy, Master Cosmo," the brainbot said. "They're made from solid titanium. It would take great strength to bend turbine blades like that. Krush must be immensely powerful."

"OK, Brain-E, I get the idea," Cosmo said, now feeling anxious. He sped past the turbine and saw more ahead, some lying toppled across the road. He drove the MAXI-truck around them, aghast at the damage the iron giant had caused.

Cosmo tried to keep his courage up, speeding after Krush in the direction of the city centre, but more signs of the invader's brutal strength became all too apparent: toppled solar towers, cracked buildings and dozens of upturned construction vehicles, including crushed loaders and cable-layers, shattered lava mixers and tow-tugs. He slowed, passing huge metal pipes rising from the ground; they had been twisted and bent too.

"These pipes bring fresh breathable air from the oxygenator," Brain-E explained.

"The oxygenator?" Cosmo asked.

"It's a structure built by Planetrax, where Syn-Nova's oxygen is made. Syn-Nova has no natural air supply, so oxygen-producing plants are grown in a vast domed structure in the city centre, and the oxygen they make is then pumped

around the planet. The oxygenator is Syn-Nova's most important structure."

"Another reason we have to stop Krush from reaching the city centre," Cosmo said.

"Watch out, Cosmo!" Nuri cried as a

Planetrax personnel carrier came speeding towards them. Cosmo swerved to avoid it and almost skidded off the road. It zoomed past, full of frightened-looking construction workers.

"They're fleeing something," Brain-E said, flashing its lights in alarm.

Cosmo heard the sound of rushing water and gasped. Up ahead a huge wave was crashing down the avenue towards the MAXI-truck.

"Uh-oh!" Nuri said. "Krush has smashed the tubular river!"

The huge overhead pipe that carried water around the city had been split, and water was gushing out, flooding the road and washing away everything in its path.

"Hold on tight!" Cosmo said, driving the MAXI-truck straight towards the wave of water. "It's bath time!"

CHAPTER FOUR

A LEAP OF FAITH

"Windows closed!" Cosmo yelled, sliding his window shut just as the wave of water hit the MAXI-truck, surging over its bonnet and cab.

With the surging water came debris from the street: street lights, road signs, paving slabs and broken glass. A turbine blade smashed straight into the MAXI, shattering its windscreen, and water began pouring inside.

"Heeelp!" Brain-E cried, as it was
washed off the dashboard.

The force of the surging water swept
the MAXI-truck into a spin, sending it
crashing against a building. Cosmo
pressed his foot down on the accelerator,
his boot splashing in the footwell,
powering the MAXI back along the
flooded street.

He swerved left and right, avoiding

debris that was washing towards them. But the closer he drove to the damaged overhead river, the stronger the surging water became, cascading from the pipe's broken end like a waterfall. Cosmo braced himself, driving the MAXI-truck beneath it. For a moment he could barely see as a solid wall of water rained down from above, thundering onto the roof and splashing into the cab.

"That's it, Cosmo! Keep going!" Nuri said encouragingly.

Cosmo drove the MAXI through the falling water and out the other side.

Brain-E bleeped, relieved. "We've made it, Master!"

But then Cosmo noticed more obstacles ahead; the avenue was blocked by huge mounds of rubble where buildings had been toppled. "Uh-oh," he said.

"Krush has annihilated this place!" Nuri exclaimed.

A dripping wet Brain-E climbed up onto the dashboard to see. "According to my data, this area is to be the city's financial district," it said.

"*Was* to be," Cosmo remarked. "It's a wreck now!"

He wrenched the MAXI-truck into first gear and drove it towards the toppled buildings. He gripped the steering wheel, shaking from side to side as the truck's wheels bounced over the rubble.

"My circuits are j-j-jangling!" Brain-E cried.

"J-j-just hold on," Cosmo said, his jaw juddering with the vibrations.

Dust swirled in the MAXI's headlights and its engine whined as Cosmo crunched through gears, driving up and over the rubble mounds.

"We'll never catch up with Krush at this rate," Nuri said.

Cosmo looked around for a quicker way through. In the rear-view mirror, he glimpsed a flash of silver from a skytrain flying low between the buildings behind.

"Maybe . . . just maybe," he muttered. He accelerated, heading up the angled wall of a fallen skyscraper, using it like a ramp.

"Cosmo, what are you doing?" Nuri asked.

"Hold on tight!" he replied, speeding faster, powering up the side of the skyscraper.

Nuri closed her eyes in fear, and

Brain-E hid in the cup holder as the MAXI-truck shot off high into the air, the skytrain speeding below.

The truck bounced down onto the skytrain's roof, and Cosmo slammed his foot on the brake, skidding to a stop.

Cosmo's knuckles were white from gripping the steering wheel, and his heart was racing so fast that he felt as if it might burst from his chest, but he'd landed the MAXI-truck safely on the skytrain – which was now speeding through the city.

"Cosmo, you're a genius!" Nuri said. "A completely crazy genius."

"Can I come out now?" Brain-E asked, peeping from the cup holder.

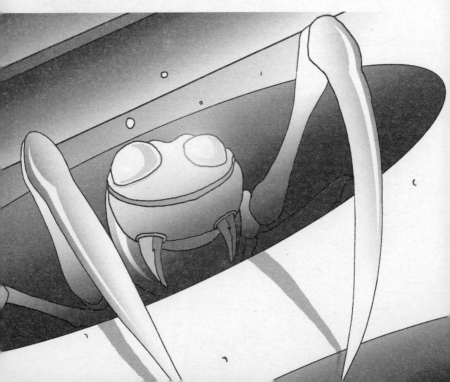

As they raced above the rubble of the ruined financial district, Cosmo looked ahead between the remaining buildings. In the distance, the sun was rising. Solar dishes glinted and the blades of wind turbines were turning in the morning breeze. Daytime was fast arriving, and with it, more skytrains came snaking between the buildings from all directions.

The city centre is filling with people for the grand opening, Cosmo realized. He shuddered, not wanting to think of what might happen with a metallicon on the rampage. *If we don't stop Krush, then their lives could be in danger!*

CHAPTER FIVE

THE OUTLAW'S PLAN

Meanwhile, far beyond the galaxy, the battleship *Oblivion* cruised the Wrecking Zone, parting a floating mass of space junk. In the ship's cockpit, the five-headed outlaw Kaos examined the monitors of a supercomputer, checking data being relayed from a special circuit board he'd implanted within the invader Krush. He was monitoring Krush's vital signs on Syn-Nova.

"His pulse is strong," Kaos's first head said, checking a spiking graph.

"And his brain waves are regular," his second head added, checking wavy lines on a screen.

Kaos's third head stared at a grainy video image. "What's that I see through Krush's optical nerves?"

"It's rubble," the fourth head said. "Krush just tore down a whole neighbourhood!"

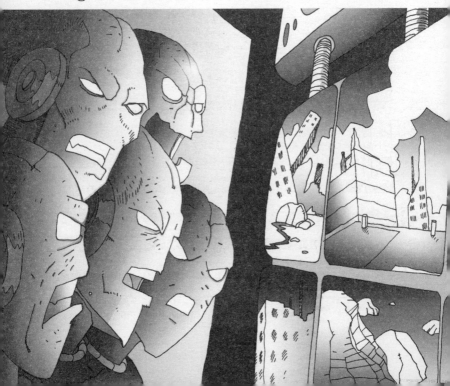

"He's unstoppable!" Kaos's fifth head exclaimed triumphantly.

"And it was *my* idea to send him into the galaxy first. Clever me!" Kaos's first head gloated. "When Krush has finished with Syn-Nova, it will be unfit for habitation. The Gamma Quadrant's expanding population will have nowhere to spread, and G-Watch will be forced to surrender to my demands."

A small purple rat scurried through the doorway and squeaked, "Eek, eek, eek!"

"What is it, Wugrat?"

"Eeeeeeek!" the rat squeaked again.

"The other metallicons are restless? They want to see me?"

Kaos strode to the cargo hold, followed by Wugrat. Inside, four huge metallicon aliens were waiting: one airborne with jet engines, another with whirring metal drills, another riding a mono-wheel and flickering with electricity, and a fourth that was armour-plated and had a cannon-arm.

"Greetings, Junkjet, Minox, Zipzap, Tanka!" Kaos said to the group.

"We want to invade!" they roared.

"Remember the deal, metal-heads," Kaos replied. "If you fight for me, you will all leave the Wrecking Zone *and* wreak havoc in the galaxy, but you must each be equipped with one of these." From a pouch on his utility belt Kaos took four small electronic circuit boards and held them up. "These I developed from stolen G-Watch android technology. Each is encoded with an invasion plan designed especially by me to match your individual talents. I will insert them into your central nervous systems to send commands to your brains."

"But I wish to leave the Wrecking Zone NOW," the jet-powered alien roared.

"All in good time, Junkjet," Kaos's second head said. "*I* have devised a *brilliant* invasion plan for you."

The alien with the spinning drill arms roared, "I want a planet to drill!"

"Patience, Minox," Kaos's third head replied. "*I* have a *deadly* plan for you."

"And what about me?" asked the metallicon flickering with electricity.

"Zipzap, *I* have a *shocking* plan for you," Kaos's fourth head said.

"Let me blast a planet to pieces," the final cannon-armed alien roared.

"Soon, Tanka, you will," the fifth head replied. "*I* have an *explosive* plan for you."

Kaos's first head addressed all four metallicons. "Let Krush signal our intent. Then each of you will join him in destruction of your own."

The metallicons' eyes blazed fiercely. "We will wait to fight for you, Master!"

There came a squeak from the back of the cargo hold, and Kaos turned to see Wugrat scurrying over. "Eek eek eek!"

"The Earthling boy?" Kaos's first head

said. Kaos picked up Wugrat by the
scruff of the neck. "Stop worrying about
him, scaredy-rat. The Earthling boy is no
match for Krush. The iron giant will
squish him dead."

Kaos flicked Wugrat away then
marched out back towards the cockpit.
"Let's watch Krush destroy Syn-Nova,"
his first head said to the others. "You will
see that *my* invasion plan is pure
genius!"

CHAPTER SIX

IT'S SHOWTIME!

Back on Syn-Nova, the MAXI-truck
hitched a ride on the roof of the skytrain
as it threaded its way between the tops
of the skyscrapers. From the MAXI's cab,
Cosmo looked down anxiously, seeing
mangled vehicles, demolished buildings
and toppled wind turbines. As they
neared the city centre, he glimpsed
people too; aliens that had come from
across the Gamma Quadrant to live on

Syn-Nova staring in shock at the damage caused to their new home.

"Where's Krush?" Cosmo said, glancing between the buildings.

"I think I can hear something," Nuri replied, her sensitive Etrusian ears twitching.

Cosmo listened hard and heard it too: the sound of vehicle horns beeping,

people shouting and sirens wailing. His Quantum Mutation Suit glowed in anticipation as he glimpsed the blue and red lights of emergency vehicles flashing up ahead. Hovercars and hoverbikes came speeding up from the streets and zoomed past in the opposite direction, dodging the MAXI-truck and skytrain.

The train let out a blast of its horn

and Cosmo gasped as he saw a huge iron alien stepping into their path. He was as tall as a building, with a body of metal machinery; one arm a hydraulic claw and the other a mighty wrecking ball. He stood on long crane legs, black smoke belching from exhaust pipes on his back.

"It's the invader Krush!" Cosmo cried. Cosmo powered up the MAXI-truck, accelerating along the skytrain towards the alien. "Nuri, open fire!"

Nuri leaned out of the window, firing at Krush with her phaser gun, but the blasts just bounced off his iron body. The huge invader reached out, grabbing the front of the skytrain with his metal claw, and swung his wrecking ball at the MAXI.

"Whoa!" Cosmo cried as the ball hit the truck, sending it flying. With a *crunch!* it hit the ground, its windows smashing as it flipped onto its roof. Cosmo and Nuri tumbled in the cab.

"Nuri, Brain-E, are you OK?" Cosmo asked.

"Just about," Nuri replied. "But we'd better get out quick."

Brain-E bleeped from the footwell. "I'm still functioning, Master Cosmo."

Cosmo managed to kick open the cab's door, and he clambered outside. Krush had the skytrain in his grasp and was crushing the front engine carriage. With the sounds of crumpling metal came screams from the passengers in the train's rear carriages.

"In the name of G-Watch, I order you to surrender!" Cosmo called to the invader.

Krush turned, his eyes flashing red as he looked down at Cosmo. "G-Watch is finished!" he roared. He tossed the skytrain aside, sending it crashing along the street, then shot out his wrecking ball at Cosmo.

Cosmo leaped out of the way just as it came smashing onto the ground beside him.

"You are no match for me!" Krush roared. Again the mighty invader swung

his wrecking ball at Cosmo, and as
Cosmo dived for cover it swept a
hovercar out of the air and demolished
the side of a building.

Cosmo summoned his courage. It was
time to use the Quantum Mutation Suit.

"SCAN!" he said into his helmet's
voice sensor. Images of aliens appeared
on the visor's digital display as the
Quantum Mutation Suit searched
through its databank: an armoured
jagon . . . a spear-tongued klatiz . . . a
swirling draxian . . .

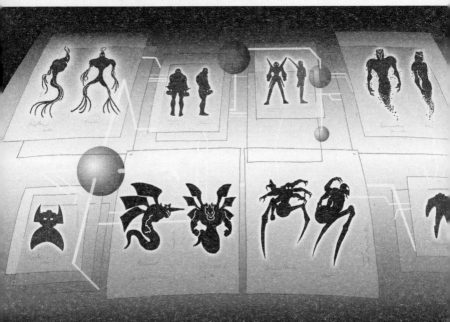

Cosmo assessed their heights, weights and features. *Which one can beat an iron giant?* he wondered. On the display appeared an image of a steaming muscular alien with piston arms.

ALIEN: PISTON
SPECIES: RAGE-TROLL
ORIGIN: THE DYDRAMOL VOLCANOES
HEIGHT: 25 METRES
WEIGHT: 9.8 TONNES
FEATURE: PISTON-POWERED PUNCH

Perfect, Cosmo thought. *Piston-powered punches will knock that iron giant to the ground.* "MUTATE!"

CHAPTER SEVEN

BANG! BANG! BAAAM!

Cosmo felt his body tingle as the
Quantum Mutation Suit fused with
his skin, reconfiguring his molecules
into those of Piston. He grew taller,
his muscles bulging and his hands
hardening into metal piston-pump fists.
Hot steam coursed through his limbs,
powering his fists, and he stomped
across the street towards Krush. "Hey,
bucket-head, leave now!" he called.

Krush turned and roared, "I take orders from no one but Kaos!"

Cosmo struck Krush with a piston-powered punch. *BANG!* Sparks flew off the invader's metal body and he staggered backwards, stepping on an abandoned hovercar and flattening it. *BANG! BANG!* Cosmo punched again and again, pummelling Krush, and the alien crumpled. *One more should do it*, Cosmo thought, tensing his muscles, building the steam power in his right arm. He blasted his fist, landing a massive right hook on Krush's chin – *BAAAM!*

Krush toppled sideways, reaching out his metal claw to stop his fall and smashing elbow-deep into a skyscraper. For a moment he leaned against the building as if finished; his face dented, a hole in his chest where a metal panel had fallen, oil dripping from a cylinder inside.

"It's over," Cosmo told him.

"I don't think so!" Krush roared back, black smoke belching from his broken exhaust pipes. He reached down, picked up the flattened hovercar and thrust it into the hole in his chest, stemming the oil leak. Cosmo stared, horrified, as the alien's metallicon flesh absorbed the vehicle into his body. *He can mend himself!* he realized.

With a roar, Krush swung his wrecking ball over his head, striking Cosmo and knocking him to the ground.

Cosmo could feel his strength fail as steam hissed from a crack in his back.

"RESET," he said. Instantly his rage-troll body began shrinking, his wounds healing as his molecules reconfigured back into those of an eleven-year-old Earthling boy.

Nuri came running over, with Brain-E clamped to her wrist for safety. "Are you OK?" she asked, helping Cosmo to his feet.

"I will be as soon as I've beaten that metal monster," Cosmo replied.

Krush was already stomping away down a wide avenue. He was heading towards a public park where citizens were gathered, waiting for the mayor to arrive for Syn-Nova's official opening. In the park's centre stood a vast, domed, multi-storey structure, each level as big as a hoverball stadium, containing thousands of plants and trees.

Cosmo gasped. *That's the oxygenator!*

he realized. *And Krush is heading
straight for it!*

As the huge alien neared the domed
oxygenator, the crowds began to flee,
screaming in panic.

Cosmo sprinted to help. "Hey, you

lump of junk – stop right there!" he shouted to Krush, but the alien paid him no attention.

"SCAN," Cosmo said into the voice sensor of his Quantum Mutation Suit. It glowed as images of aliens appeared again on its visor's digital display.

He saw a fear-twisting hervon . . . a microtoxic ploxia . . . a screeching vargo . . . and settled on an image of a freakish-looking alien with long jointed legs and spider-eyes.

ALIEN: ARAN
SPECIES: SPIDRAX
ORIGIN: THE USRAN COMET FIELDS
HEIGHT: 12.3 METRES
WEIGHT: 1.2 TONNES
FEATURE: STEEL WEB SPINNER

A steel web should hold that invader, Cosmo thought. "MUTATE!"

CHAPTER EIGHT

A STICKY SOLUTION

Cosmo felt his body tingle as his molecules reconfigured into those of Aran. His eyes bulged from his face, green and glassy, and his body grew larger, his legs lengthening and two extra pairs of arms pushing out from his sides. He felt web-spinning glands opening on the palms of his hands, oozing a sticky metallic substance.

He raced after Krush, leaping ten metres with each long stride. *Cool,* he thought. *Aran is super-fast*. He tried his web-spinners, flexing his fingers and shooting steel cables down the street, swinging from building to building in pursuit of the invader. All around, alien citizens were fleeing from the iron giant. Krush stomped among them, swatting a hovercar away with his metal claw, then striding into the park and whacking an information screen with his wrecking ball, sending it flying. Cosmo shot out cables, catching the hovercar and the information screen, then laying them safely on the ground.

Krush approached the oxygenator and swung his wrecking ball round and round, faster and faster, about to smash it into the huge glass dome.

"No you don't!" Cosmo yelled. He fired steel webs at the ball as it swung through the air. They caught it and he tugged, pulling the huge ball of iron towards him.

"What is this?" Krush roared, trying to yank his wrecking ball free.

"A little tangled, are you?" Cosmo called. He shot out more steel cables then raced around the alien again and again, binding him like a fly in a web. "You're not welcome in this city, Krush!"

"Enough!" Krush roared. Angrier than ever, he stoked up his engines, causing them to belch black smoke. His hydraulic claw began to rip and tear at the cables, breaking them. The iron giant burst free, then jabbed his claw at Cosmo, who went flying into the side of the oxygenator. He slid down the glass wall to the ground, dazed.

"RESET!" he gasped, turning back into a boy in the Quantum Mutation Suit.

The iron giant loomed over him, his wrecking ball raised. "Prepare to be crushed, G-Watch weakling!"

All of a sudden Cosmo heard the clatter

of caterpillar tracks. A bulldozer came speeding across the park with Nuri at the wheel and drove straight into Krush.

"Aaargh!" the alien roared as the bulldozer shunted him backwards.

"I thought you could do with some help, Cosmo," Nuri called from the cab.

Cosmo smiled with relief. "You're just in time!" he yelled back.

Nuri reversed the bulldozer, then rammed Krush again, pushing the invader away from the oxygenator.

"Get off me!" he roared with fury.

Cosmo saw Brain-E scuttle out of the bulldozer's cab onto Krush's metal leg and undo screws on a panel. The invader's kneecap fell off!

"Nice one, Brain-E!" Cosmo called.

But Krush merely roared and shook the brainbot off, then reached for the bulldozer with his demolition claw.

As Nuri crunched the gears and accelerated, trying to ram him again, Krush closed his claw around the bulldozer, picking it up. He crushed it like a can: its caterpillar tracks fell off and its windscreen shattered.

Nuri scrambled out of the cab and leaped to safety.

"Syn-Nova is history!" Krush roared. He strode back towards Cosmo and the oxygenator, swinging his wrecking ball above his head, then unleashing it. The blow landed just metres away from Cosmo on the side of the oxygenator, cracking its reinforced dome . . .

CHAPTER NINE

INVISIBLE STRENGTH

The mighty alien swung his wrecking ball at the oxygenator again, smashing a hole in its dome. "I will destroy this thing," he roared. "And with no oxygen to breathe, all life on Syn-Nova will perish."

"SCAN," Cosmo said into his helmet's sensor. On the visor, images of more aliens appeared. *What is a match for a metal giant?* he thought desperately. He saw an image of a pulsing silver alien . . .

```
ALIEN: MAGNETRON
SPECIES: IONIZER
ORIGIN: PLANET FERRUS
LENGTH: 22.8 METRES
WEIGHT: 10 TONNES
FEATURES: MAGNETIC STRENGTH
```

Magnetic strength could be just the thing! "MUTATE!" he yelled.

Immediately Cosmo began to transform into Magnetron. He grew powerful, his skin hardening to a shine. He felt his muscles ripple, then pulse, magnetism radiating from his body.

As Krush swung his wrecking ball at the oxygenator, trying to open up the hole he'd smashed, Cosmo reached out towards the alien with his magnetic hands and instantly Krush's wrecking ball stopped in mid-air.

The invader stared, confused. "What is this invisible strength you possess?" he roared.

Magnetron's magnetic force was pulling the wrecking ball back, stopping it from

striking the oxygenator's glass! Cosmo
focused all his magnetic strength onto the
iron wrecking ball, heaving it away from
the oxygenator. Krush roared, trying to
yank it back. The two aliens were locked
in a battle of strength: magnetic versus
mechanical. The links in the chain holding

the wrecking ball began to bend and break under the strain.

Suddenly the chain snapped and the wrecking ball dropped to the ground.

"What have you done to me?" Krush roared angrily.

"Give up," Cosmo ordered.

"Never!" Instead the alien plunged his massive metal claw through the crack in the oxygenator's shell and started ripping out the plants.

Cosmo flexed his muscles again, increasing his magnetic strength, focusing on Krush's metal body parts. Bolts began to pop out, attracted by the magnetism. *Pop! Pop! Pop!* One of the pincers of his huge claw fell off. *Pop! Pop! Pop!* The bolts in his torso sprang out and panels flew from his chest, exposing a huge, filthy engine inside. He was breaking apart! *Pop! Pop! Pop!* One of his big iron feet fell off his leg, and the iron

giant stumbled. Magnetron was more
than a match for him!

"Aargh!" the invader raged, his jaw
dropping as its hinges pinged off.

"RESET!" Cosmo said, and instantly
his magnetic body shrank as he turned
back into a boy again.

Krush fell to the ground, his eyes
blazing red with anger.

"You've caused enough destruction,

Krush," Cosmo said. "Now it's time for you to leave this planet."

"As long as I have metal in my veins, I will fight on!" the alien roared.

"Not any more!" The Quantum Mutation Suit glowed brightly as the power of the universe surged inside Cosmo. White and blue light burst from his gloved hand – his power taking the physical form of a sword. "The power of the universe is in me!" he called, rushing

over to the invader. He wielded the power sword and it struck the metallicon like a bolt of lightning.

A deep roar rose from within Krush's engine. "NOOOOOOOOOOO!"

For a moment Cosmo's power was locked in battle with the invader's, every molecule of his body fighting Krush's destructive rage, trying to neutralize him.

The alien's engine sputtered, and in a blast of dirty black smoke he exploded.

Cosmo collapsed, breathless with exhaustion and relief.

"Cosmo, that was amazing!" he heard. It was Nuri, running over with Brain-E on her wrist, the brainbot's lights flashing.

"Master Cosmo, I knew you could do it!"

"Not without you guys," he said, smiling.

As he was helped to his feet by Nuri, he heard the sirens of Planetrax emergency vehicles coming to repair the oxygenator's dome. "We should get back to the Dragster and let G1 know that Syn-Nova is safe," he said.

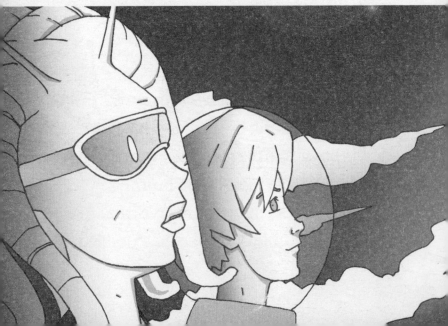

"Thank you," a voice called from above. It was the frog-faced Mayor of Syn-Nova, arriving in a stately hovercar to open the city. He raised his right hand, saluting Cosmo. "On behalf of the people of Syn-Nova, is there any way I can repay you?"

Cosmo smiled. "I don't suppose you could give us a lift back to our spaceship, could you?"

CHAPTER TEN

A SECOND ATTEMPT

In the cockpit of the battleship *Oblivion*, Wugrat squeaked frantically.

Kaos ran in, alarmed. "What's that you say, Wugrat? Krush shut down?" his first head cried in disbelief.

All five heads glared at the digital monitors relaying the invader's vital signs. The graph that had previously been spiking was now flat-lining.

"Pulse zero," Kaos's second head said.

On the next screen the wavy lines were now still. "Brain waves non-existent," Kaos's third head added.

"And look! This is the final signal from Krush's optical nerves," his fourth head said, pointing to a grainy image of an Earthling boy, a power sword in his hand.

Kaos's fifth head sneered, "The G-Watch shrimp beat him!"

"B-b-but this is impossible!" the first head spluttered.

The other four heads glared at the first, eight eyes against two. "It seems your plan wasn't so 'genius' after all!"

"Blasted G-Watch!" Kaos's first head spat. "It must have been a fluke!"

"It's *my* turn now," the second head said. "Unleash the next invader! The plan that *I* have created is sure to work."

Kaos hurried into the cargo hold, where the four remaining alien invaders were waiting. "Junkjet, you're needed!"

The flying alien swooped down and Kaos dragged a ladder over from the side of the cargo hold. He leaned it against Junkjet, then picked up a laser saw and climbed up.

"Now bend your head down while I implant your orders," Kaos's second head told the alien.

Junkjet leaned forward and Kaos turned the laser saw on. A white-hot laser beam shot out of it.

"This may hurt a little," Kaos's second head told him. "In fact, it may hurt a lot."

"Metallicons feel no pain," Junkjet replied.

Kaos aimed the laser cutter, and it burned into the top of Junkjet's head, slicing through the metal. He peeled back the casing like the lid of a tin can, exposing throbbing metallic flesh. Then, from his utility belt, he took one of the four

remaining computerized circuit boards.

"Hold still now," he said, thrusting the circuit board elbow-deep inside. With a sucking sound, it sank into the alien's soft metallic flesh, and in a sparking flash, Junkjet's metallicon innards absorbed the wires and microchips. Kaos replaced the metal on the invader's head and the metallicon flesh bubbled up like mercury, soldering the wound shut.

"On that circuit board is an invasion plan especially designed by *me*," Kaos's second head said.

Junkjet raised his head, his eyes flashing menacingly. "Plan understood, Master," he replied. "I will not fail."

Kaos climbed back down the ladder, grinning. "Wugrat, where's the navicom?"

The little rat scurried over with a crystal navicom transporter disc in his mouth. Kaos snatched it from him, then twisted the outer edge like a dial. He attached it to Junkjet, and the navicom began flashing. "Junkjet, do your fiercest," Kaos said to the invader.

Junkjet's engines roared as the roof of the cargo hold opened. A blue light began to glow from the navicom, and with a *whoosh!* Junkjet shot out of the battleship, vanishing into space.

* * *

By the time Cosmo, Nuri and Brain-E reached the Dragster, the sun was high in the sky. All across Syn-Nova, Planetrax construction crews were out repairing the damage caused by Krush, and more and more skytrains were arriving, bringing new citizens to the city.

Cosmo and Nuri said goodbye to the Mayor and climbed aboard the Dragster. Cosmo pressed a button on the communications console, connecting to G-Watch headquarters, and G1's face appeared on the screen.

"Krush has been defeated," Cosmo told him. "He tried to take out Syn-Nova's oxygen supply to destroy the planet, but we stopped him in time. Syn-Nova is safe."

The silver-eyed chief smiled. "Congratulations, Cosmo. Thousands of lives have been saved, thanks to you."

"It was a team effort," Cosmo told him, glancing at Nuri and Brain-E.

Nuri smiled. "Cosmo's just being modest," she said. "He pulled that iron giant to pieces."

G1's brow furrowed. "I hate to ruin the celebrations, but our scanners have detected a second invader being beamed into the galaxy. He's heading towards the Starflight Spaceship Manufacturing Company in the Delta Quadrant. We've identified him as a flying metallicon known as Junkjet."

"We're on to it," Cosmo replied.

"Good luck, Cosmo," G1 said. "The power of the universe is in you."

"Thanks, G1."

It felt good to be back at the helm of the Dragster. Cosmo powered up the spaceship's thrusters and took off from Syn-Nova. Glancing down, he saw the construction crews and vehicles at work, and skytrains bringing in more citizens. *Thanks to G-Watch, Syn-Nova will prosper and grow now*, he thought proudly. *And its citizens are safe.* "Nuri, set a course for the Delta Quadrant. Junkjet, here we come!"

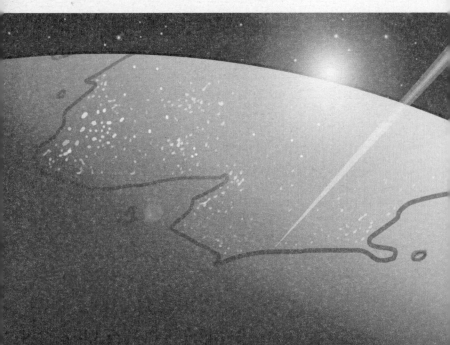

Join Cosmo on his next **ALIEN INVADERS**
mission. He must face – and defeat

JUNKJET
THE FLYING MENACE

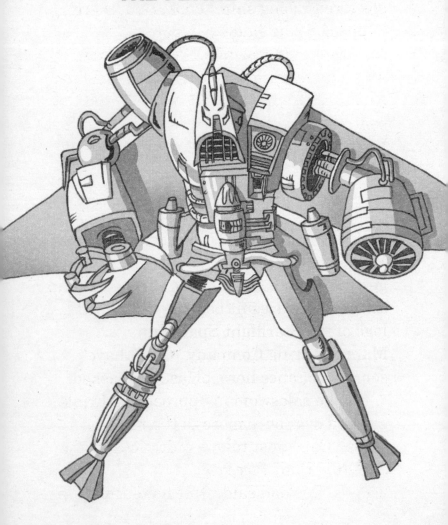

INVADER ALERT!

In a glass-domed spaceship showroom in the Noverian Orb Fields, Frink Blatter pointed one of his hairy Ubliac arms to a sleek red racing ship. "Look, Dad, there's a Zephron 8!" he said excitedly.

Frink's dad frowned. "We're not buying a Zephron, Frink." He stepped instead to a saucer-ship with a bubble cockpit in its centre. "How about this Moonbeam Reliable? I've heard it's very fuel-efficient." Then he ran his hand along the fin of a white wagonship. "Or maybe a Roomstar?"

"Are they fast, Dad?" Frink asked.

"We don't need a fast spaceship, Frink. We need something practical." His dad gestured to a bald Riverian saleswoman in an orange spacesuit bearing the SSMC logo of the Starflight Spaceship Manufacturing Company. "Can I have some assistance here, please?" he asked.

As the saleswoman approached, Frink glanced over once more to the racing ships. "Can I just take a quick look at the Zephron, Dad? *Pleeease.*"

"OK," his dad said. "But no touching."

"I won't!" Frink ran across the domed showroom, past microships and toolships to the racing ships section. The Zephron looked even better up close: a single-seater arrowhead rocketship in racing red. He glanced back, checking that his dad and the saleswoman weren't watching, then climbed up into its cockpit and dropped into the pilot seat. The cockpit hood closed automatically over his head and he gripped the steering column. *Awesome!*

Frink looked up through the showroom's glass dome into space, pretending he was flying. He spotted an object flying down towards the showroom. *Probably another customer,* he thought. *I'd better get out.* But the object was coming in too fast to be a customer in a spaceship. *Whoa! Way too fast!*

There came the sound of breaking glass as a massive machine smashed through the dome into the showroom. Frink buried his head in his hands, debris clattering against the Zephron's hull. He peered out at the wreckage: spaceships lying upturned and mangled, fragments of glass everywhere. *Dad,* Frink thought, concerned. In all the confusion, he couldn't see if his Dad was safe.

Then he heard the roar of a jet engine and gasped as the machine rose from the showroom floor. It was some kind of freak alien, unlike anything he'd ever seen before: a huge living machine with wings and jets.

Time to get out of here, Frink thought, fumbling for the release switch to the cockpit hood. But in his panic, he hit the wrong one. The Zephron's control panel lit up and an electronic voice sounded, "Launch mode commencing . . ." The ship's nose tilted upwards, "Preparing for blast-off . . ." Frink gulped, not knowing what to do; he had never flown a spaceship before. "Have a safe flight," the computerized voice said, the Zephron's fins extending from its sides. Frink saw the freakish machine-like alien coming for him. As the Zephron's thrusters ignited, the alien swiped a large metal claw, striking it with a *CLANG!*

"I am Junkjet!" the alien roared. "And I'm here to tear this place apart!"

CHAPTER ONE
COLLISION COURSE

"Look at me! I'm flying, Master Cosmo!"

Cosmo chuckled as the ship's brainbot, Brain-E, came whizzing through the Dragster 7000's cockpit, wearing a new copter-blade attachment that it had found on the kit shelf. "Way to go, Brain-E!" Cosmo said.

The brainbot circled the navigation console, then tried a loop-the-loop, knocking into the spacescreen and ricocheting off the steering column. It landed with a *bump!* on the control desk. "Oops!"

"Don't worry, Brain-E, you'll soon get the hang of it," Cosmo said encouragingly.

"I hope so. This could come in handy on our mission, Master Cosmo."

Cosmo smiled, glad to have Brain-E with him.

"Look sharp, you two. In ten seconds we exit hyperdrive," interrupted Agent Nuri, Cosmo's Etrusian co-pilot. She unscrewed Brain-E's copter attachment and Cosmo took the Dragster's controls, counting down in his head. *Ten . . . nine . . . eight . . .*

They were blasting along Hyperway 62 on a dangerous mission for the galactic security force, G-Watch. Five alien invaders were being beamed into the galaxy by the evil outlaw Kaos, and it was down to Cosmo and his team to stop them. Cosmo had already defeated the first of them: Krush the iron giant, and was now speeding to the galaxy's Delta Quadrant to fight the second invader: Junkjet. G-Watch scanners had identified the alien beaming towards the headquarters of the Starflight Spaceship Manufacturing Company there.

. . . *three . . . two . . . one . . .* Cosmo flicked a silver switch then turned the steering column, feeling his ears pop as the spaceship veered off the hyperway. He slowed to seven vectrons, and stars reappeared in the spacescreen. Directly ahead he saw a cluster of shining planets with syphon ships docked alongside.

"Those planets are called the Noverian Orbs," Nuri said. "The Starflight Company uses them."

"Uses them? For what?"

"To build spaceships from. They're

planets of molten metal from which raw materials are extracted by syphon ship."

On the spacescreen a message flashed up: STARFLIGHT TERRITORY — ACCESS RESTRICTED.

"Access restricted – how come?" Cosmo asked.

Brain-E bleeped from the control desk. "The Starflight Spaceship Manufacturing Company occupies this whole region. There is an open-access spaceway to its public showroom but all other areas are off-limits on account of its hazardous test zone and top-secret factory. Starflight is one of the galaxy's largest companies, building millions of spaceships every year."

"And G-Watch scanners picked up Junkjet heading this way," Cosmo replied, concerned. "OK, Brain-E, what do we know about this alien?"

The brainbot's lights flashed as it searched its databank for information. "G-Watch reconnaissance probes from the Wrecking Zone record this alien as a winged assassin capable of tearing to pieces any vessel in its path."

"Well, if Junkjet tries anything on us, we'll send him back to his junkyard!"

Cosmo said defiantly. His courage grew and his spacesuit began to glow.

Cosmo was wearing the Quantum Mutation Suit, a living body armour with which he could mutate into awesome alien forms. It was activated by the power of the universe – a power present in all living things, but uniquely strong in Cosmo.

"Get ready," Nuri said, checking the navigation console. "According to scanner data, Junkjet beamed in somewhere around here."

Cosmo reduced power to the thrusters as he flew past another orb attended by Starflight syphon ships. Suddenly a light flashed on the communications console indicating an incoming message.

"It's an open frequency broadcast from another spaceship," Nuri said, flicking a switch to open the channel.

"Help! Somebody help me!" they heard a panicked voice say over the airwaves. "I can't fly this thing!"

It sounds like a boy's voice, Cosmo thought. "Send a reply, Nuri," he said.

Nuri connected to the frequency. "This is G-Watch in the Dragster 7000. Please state your name and location."

"My name's Frink Blatter," a voice replied. "And I'm aaar—'

"Spaceship incoming, Master Cosmo," Brain-E interrupted, pointing its metal leg to the Dragster's radar screen. A light on the display indicated a spaceship coming straight towards them at high speed.

Cosmo quickly turned the steering column to avoid a collision as a Zephron 8 racing ship appeared and shot past like a speeding dart. It was hurtling towards one of the molten metal orbs where the syphon ships were at work. Cosmo gasped. "It's out of control!"

Brain-E's lights flashed as the brainbot ran a calculation. "And on a course to collide with that orb in precisely seventy-six Earth seconds."

Cosmo banked the Dragster and increased speed, racing after the Zephron. "Frink, this is Cosmo Santos in the Dragster 7000," he radioed. "I'm coming after you. Steer away from those orbs."

"But there's something wrong with this thing's steering," Frink replied. "And I can't seem to slow it down either!"

Flying at high speed, Cosmo brought the Dragster closer to the Zephron.

"One of its flaps is damaged and the hull's badly ripped," Nuri said, peering through the spacescreen. "I can see broken cabling too."

Cosmo glimpsed a hairy Ubliac boy in the Zephron's cockpit, his arms trembling as he tried to fly the stricken spaceship.

"Frink, you've got to reduce speed now and change course or you're going to collide with that orb straight ahead," Cosmo instructed over the communicator.

"I'm trying, but the steering column won't budge," the boy replied, panic rising in his voice.

Nuri turned to Cosmo. "The damage to the Zephron's cabling could have jammed its controls," she told him.

The Zephron was hurtling closer to the molten metal planet.

"Direct impact in forty-nine seconds," Brain-E said.

"Help!" Frink yelled over the airwaves.

"OK, Nuri, take the controls," Cosmo told her, unbuckling his flying harness and leaving his seat. "Fly us directly above the

Zephron. I'm going to try and pull Frink out of there."

"At this speed? Are you crazy?"

"We have no choice. In about forty seconds the Zephron will hit that orb and explode, and Frink and any workers on those syphon ships will go up in a fireball." Cosmo swallowed an oxygen pill, then closed his helmet's visor.

"Thirty-eight seconds now, Master Cosmo," Brain-E said.

Cosmo quickly dropped into the Dragster's airlock and closed the hatch behind him. He attached himself to the space-walk harness, checking its safety cable was firmly secured to the Dragster, then he opened the airlock's external hatch. They were flying directly above the Zephron.

"That's it, Nuri, hold us steady," he said into his helmet mic. He focused, summoning the power inside him, then took a deep breath and jumped.

**Find out what happens in
JUNKJET – THE FLYING MENACE . . .**